The Mystery Adventures of Charlotte Holmes

Ben Richards

DEDICATED TO

Our friends in Saddleworth, Market Drayton, Huddersfield and Lancaster who have been with us on our adventures from the very beginning.

This book tells some of the same stories as the Charlotte Holmes Adventure Box.

If you would like to play the Charlotte Holmes Adventure Box **before** reading this book, please visit www.charlotteholmes.co.uk

WARNING: knowing the ending cannot be undone!

CONTENTS

1 THE GOING AWAY PRESENT

Thursday 31st August 1939

Dear Diary,

I am being evacuated from London tomorrow. I am very excited.

Mr Bowman says it isn't safe for children in London in case we go to war. All of us are getting moved to the country. Mr Bowman told me the children from our school are being sent to Yorkshire… wherever that is!

And he said I get to go on the train! I've never been on a train before. It's going to feel so strange. I bet people will think I'm posh.

I raced through all my chores so I could pack my bags.

I didn't have much to pack, just some clothes and my diary.

Mum has taped in a photo inside the case. It's her and dad on the day they were married. She says this way they'll be in Yorkshire with me. That's stupid. I told her, "It doesn't matter where the photo is – you'll still be in London and Dad will still be dead."

I told her to take it back, but she wouldn't have it. She said she didn't want me to forget what she looked like.

How could I? She's looks like me. Mum comes from Jamaica. She met dad when he went there on business. They moved to England after they got married. Mum says that's why I look half-Jamaican and half-English. I think I just look like me... and I feel British through and through.

Once I had packed, I went out to play with my friends.

Mum said, "Don't be late for supper, Charlotte. It'll be our last supper together for a while."

Mum is always being silly like that.

I felt like saying: "What does it matter? We've had a million suppers together already."

But I wanted to be quick so I just said, "I won't be late, Mum," and went out to play.

I had to hunt a bit before I found anybody. They were all in the brewery yard.

There was Herbie from next-door - he turned eleven last week; Dora who's nine; and the twins David and Susan – they're both ten and a half, but Susan tells everyone she was born first so she's the big sister.

They were all playing with a new whip and top that Herbie's aunt had given to him.

"It's a going away present," Herbie explained. "It's something to play with in Yorkshire."

I wish I had an aunt like Herbie's. She always has money to spend on him. It isn't fair really. We are all being evacuated at the same time – nobody has given me a going away present. It isn't my fault my mum is so poor.

The whip and top is a funny toy. You spin the wooden top till it's going really fast and you try to keep it going by whipping it with a piece of leather on a stick.

Dora's the best at it. She can keep it doing for ages. Most of the time I ended up missing, or I whip it into the cobbles where it gets stuck.

We must have been playing for ever so long, because before we knew it, the sun had gone down and Dora's mum came and gave her an earful.

"Dora Babbage – I've been worried sick. Don't you think with your dad away in the army I've enough to be worried about? You were supposed to come home three hours ago."

"Poor Dora," I thought "I'm glad my mum doesn't shout like that." But just as I thought it, Dora's mum turned around and started to shout at me too.

"You're the oldest, Charlotte Holmes. You should be responsible. But you're just a waste of space." Dora's mum is not very nice. Her tongue darts in and out when she speaks. It makes her look like a venomous snake.

She poked me with her long, bony finger.

"I told you, I don't want you playing with Dora – You're a bad influence. I don't want my Dora turning out like you, Charlotte Holmes. No Holmes will ever amount to anything – mark my words."

David and Susan tried to stick up for me, but Dora's mum has a much louder voice than both of them together. She just carried on talking and wagging her finger.

"The rest of you – shoo! Your mums will be waiting up. Come on, Dora – we're going home."

And with that, she pinched poor little Dora by the ear and dragged her off back to the terraces.

I walked with Herbie. He said he bets Dora is over the moon to be evacuated. She probably is. I would be if my mum was mean like hers.

When we got back it was really late. I had completely forgotten about dinner. Mum was sat at the table, looking at old photos of her and Dad in Jamaica. She had tears in her eyes.

"You missed our last supper," she said without looking up.

I told her it wasn't my fault. I said about Herbie's going away whip and top. I told her if she had bought me a going away present I would have stayed home to play with it. I told her if I had a present I wouldn't have missed the last supper. I told her if anyone was to blame it was her. She was a bad mother. I'm glad I missed supper. I can't wait till tomorrow – I'll be happier when she's not there.

Then I stopped.

I realised what a terrible thing I had said. I didn't mean those things really. I don't even know why I said them.

But Mum didn't shout back at me. Mum didn't say anything. She just reached out and put a small parcel on the table. It said on the label:

"To Charlotte, I got a going away present. I'll miss you, love Mum."

I felt like there were stones in my belly.

She had covered the wrapping all over with pictures. She'd coloured them in too. It must have taken her ages.

"Sorry," I said. "It's nice. Shall I open it?"

"Do as you please," Mum replied. "I'm going to bed. Make sure you turn out the lights. Be quick."

Then she left. She didn't even kiss me goodnight.

I opened the present.

It's a box of mikado.

I've been saying I want mikado for ages.

I should feel happy. I don't.

I think I'm a terrible person.

2 EVACUEE

Friday 1st September 1939

11am

Dear Diary,

I had a dippy egg for breakfast.

Mum got up early and bought us fresh bread. She didn't seem cross like I thought she would be. We talked about Yorkshire, Germany and the Prime Minister. They said on the radio that the Germans had invaded Poland. Mum said we'll go to war if the Germans don't leave Poland. I hope they do. War doesn't sound very fun.

As soon as we'd finished, we put on our coats and walked across London to Euston Station.

When we arrived, a man at a desk checked my name on the register. Then, he wrote my name really big on a label and tied it around my neck. It looks stupid, but I'm not allowed to take it off till I get to Yorkshire.

Inside, the station was crammed full of children: some very small, some older than me.

Everybody was chattering, fussing and saying goodbye to one another. It was ever so loud.

Mum squeezed us through to the front of the platform so I would be one of the first on the carriage when the doors opened.

The train is amazing. It's every bit as impressive as I imagined it would be: so black and so shiny - and big – it's enormous! When you stand very close, you can't even see the front end.

I told Mum I was sorry. She said she forgave me. She told me she loved me. I told her I loved her too and she gave me a hug and a kiss on the cheek.

Then the train whistle blew and the carriage doors opened.

There was an almighty crush. Everyone wanted to be first on the train. I tried, but elbows kept bumping me back. Someone knocked my case from my hand, and I got kicked in the head when I bent down to pick it up.

In the end Mum had to push in herself. She lifted me up to the step. Before I could turn to say bye, I was pushed right inside as a whole bunch more people squeezed their way in.

There were still a few seats left but none on the platform side. I put my bag on an empty seat, and tried to squeeze through to the other side. I wanted to wave through the window. We promised we'd wave to each other. But the crowding was as bad in the train as it was on the platform. Bigger boys hogged all the platform side windows. I kept getting jostled away.

I asked them: "Excuse me. Can I wave to my mum?" But nobody moved.

Next thing, the whistle blew. The train started moving.

All I could see were the backs of other children waving goodbye to their families. Mum mustn't have known where to wave. I had to keep trying…

Eventually I managed to find a spot, but by then the train was well out of the station. The platform was so far away, all the people were dots. I'd missed her. I'd missed out our wave.

That thought made me sad.

I did a little wave at the dots in the distance, just to say that I had.

The boy sat by the window laughed. He said no-one could see me. There's no point in waving. I'm wasting my time. And could I get away from his seat.

"Yeah, well you're stupid. I'll stand where I want." That's what I could have said.

That's what I thought.

I might have said it too – just…

He was so old (14 perhaps).

I was so sad.

And he was right – No-one could see me. There really was no point.

I went to my seat and sat down.

5pm

Dear Diary,

What a wonderful day!

So much has happened. I can barely believe it's the same day I left London.

I'm writing this lying in my own four poster bed. In my own room. With my own wash basin and my own mirror. I've so much to tell you – and the day isn't over yet.

When the train pulled into Huddersfield, the train guard led us out one by one all in a line.

A lady with a blue hat checked off our names on a list.

We all had to stand in a group near the ticket office. There must have been hundreds of children there, everyone chatting and joking. It was very exciting.

Out in the reception area, there was another crowd, only all grown-ups. Word went round they were to be our new "parents". Some kids looked nervous, but I wasn't. I've never been shy at all with new people.

Murmuring started. All of us children started picking out our favourites. Everyone wanted someone who looked kind. Someone well dressed – and not so very old.

Margaret, a girl who I met on the train said she was basically grown-up, nearly 15, and she'd only be taken in by a tall handsome man. Or else, she said she'd evacuate straight back to London. She'd picked out a youngish man right near the back and kept doing waves at him, mouthing "pick me".

The lady marshal slapped the back of her hands. She told her to stop – said she'd go where they sent her and not to try their patience. Margaret looked very embarrassed. She didn't dare wave to any grown-ups after that.

One funny thing was: the grown-ups didn't seem excited like we were. Most of them didn't look pleased to be there. In fact, from the look of them, most of them looked like they'd rather not be there – or have an evacuee at all.

One by one, grown-ups came up, and told one of the marshals how many children they'd take, and whether they'd take girls or boys.

The marshals shouted out names from the list and if they shouted yours you had to go over. Mostly the grown-ups just smiled and took their evacuees home.

Sometimes, they'd pull a face and say something like "Oh no, that one's far too fat, give me another," or "That one's got glasses. I don't want one with glasses." Then the children just sidled back to the crowd.

It happened a few times.

It happened to me. Not once but four times.

I couldn't hear what any of them said to the marshal. There was lots of whispering and looking me up and down.

Soon there was only me left at the station. All of the adults had left.

The lady marshal was terribly kind.

She made up a whole bunch of reasons why I was left over. Not one of them was the fact nobody wanted me.

She said she'd ring round. Find an emergency home for me. Then try again next week when the next train came in.

But while she was speaking, a big car pulled up: sparkling, gleaming from bonnet to fenders, and a very smart, very well dressed man got out. He was quite young and he had a very handsome thin moustache that made him look important. He was smiling and whistling a merry little tune to himself.

Whoever he was, the lady marshal recognised him immediately. She told me to stay put and went over to meet him.

They were quite far away and I struggled to hear them. He was saying he was sorry… something about a flat tyre. Then he asked if he'd missed everything.

The lady marshal nodded.

I shuffled closer.

The man spoke in a low voice with a funny kind of accent. It sounded so different from people in London. "Drat – what a pity. We were so looking forward to having an evacuee. And now everyone's picked."

"I've not been picked," I said, poking my head round the corner.

He pointed at me. "Who's that?" he asked.

The lady marshal looked at her clipboard and answered, "Charlotte Holmes. She's down for emergency accommodation."

When he heard that, the man looked rather cross. "Whatever for? We've got a room ready. Come over here, Charlotte. My name's Johnson. Tell me - how are you finding Yorkshire so far?"

I told him so far I liked everything, except not being picked. That bit wasn't much fun.

He smiled, but the lady marshal said "If you prefer, you could come back next week – you'll have plenty more choice. I could give you first pick."

Straight away Johnson said, "Why would I do that? My first pick would be Charlotte Holmes. I think she's quite the best evacuee. Would you like to come back with me, Charlotte?" He asked.

I said yes. And double quick, he grabbed my case and my hand and in no time at all we were driving away in the fabulous car.

He drove ever so fast. It was so exciting to watch all the scenery rush by. We were driving for ages, but I didn't mind. He taught me the tune he was whistling, and by the time we got to where we were going I could whistle it almost as well as him.

We arrived at the house – a great big mansion! It's called Batley Hall and now I live there too!

It isn't his house though. It's really Sir Jeremy Batley's.

Johnson is Sir Jeremy's driver. Fancy that - having your own private driver!

And that's not all – since then I've met the maid, Alice – she's funny. She's twenty years old and she's really pretty. She talks at a hundred miles an hour: she told me all about how she keeps her long brown hair so shiny, and how she hates having to hide it under her little maid's hat. I met her as she was trying to sneak into the kitchen for biscuits. She said not to tell on her - cross my heart and hope to die. I promised. I like her.

And there's Alfred, Sir Jeremy's butler. He's tall, plump and ever so bald. He's strict too! He didn't smile once when he showed me my room. Maybe he's shy around new people. I'll just remember to be extra nice to him – I'm sure he'll be friendly when he gets to know me.

I'm going to meet Sir Jeremy now. How strange – to meet a REAL SIR! It sounds very posh. I hope that he's nice. Fingers crossed!

3 THE MYSTERY OF THE BROKEN BISCUIT BARREL

Saturday 2nd September 1939

2pm

Dear Diary,

Sir Jeremy's lovely. He's good through and through. You can see it as soon as you look in his eyes.

Sir Jeremy has very kind eyes - the type of eyes that only see the very best in other people – and his hair is going grey at the sides. Mum says grey hair is a sign of wisdom (she's said it a few times since she noticed in the mirror that a few of her own hairs had turned!)

He was wearing a smoking jacket, a silk scarf and tiny little glasses that were barely balanced on top of his nose. He had the most beautiful study I have ever seen. The walls were covered in oak panels and there a huge stone fire place next to Sir Jeremy's arm chair.

He gave me a book called 'THE MYSTERY ADVENTURES

OF SHERLOCK HOLMES' – the greatest detective there ever was.

How funny! We have the same surname.

I tried to start chapter one last night, but it's covered in scribbles: scribbles in the margin, scribbles inside the covers.

Some are just words. Some are full paragraphs. Some even have diagrams. But they're ever so tiny. Thank goodness Sir Jeremy gave me a magnifying glass, or I might have gone blind trying to read them all.

In the end, I spent so long trying to puzzle out the scribbles I fell asleep before I read any of the stories. I'll have another go tonight. I'll read one case a night and I'll finish in no time.

I met some more people after Sir Jeremy.

Henry – he's my age. He's really good fun. He always wants to play games and do exciting things. We played a game of mikado yesterday. He beat me three times. But I'm going to practice!

Ralph the dog – he's Sir Jeremy's Border Collie.

I've never lived in a house with a dog before.

He has the most gorgeous fur, it's amazing for stroking. I like his soft sticky-up ears, they feel nice and velvety, and he loves it when you scratch them.

Henry and I took Ralph out for a walk this morning. He dashed up and down and all through the flowerbeds! For a little while both of us lost him. It took ages to find him, and when we did, he was digging up turnips from the vegetable patch! Thank goodness Doug the groundsman didn't see him. I've not met Doug yet, but I bet he'll be cross when he sees what Ralph's done.

I wasn't.

I don't think I could ever be cross with that dog, I love him so much. When I grow up I'm going to have twenty dogs, all just like Ralph.

When we came back I met Henry's mum, Mrs Mirfield. She cooks Sir Jeremy's food, and everyone else's. It's really delicious.

Today she was baking. She's making some cakes for Batley fête. She even let me help. She gave me some recipes.

Mrs Mirfield says baking is a panacea.

That's a funny word, I thought. I looked it up in the dictionary, it says:

Panacea

A solution or remedy for all difficulties or diseases.

Mrs Mirfield says, no matter what your problems are, they all melt away when you start baking.

Henry's dad, Mr Mirfield, didn't live at Batley Hall all the time. He was a sailor in the Royal Navy. Henry said if we go to war, his dad's boat will be on the front line. Mrs Mirfield turns up the radio when the news comes on. They must be so worried. No wonder she loves doing baking so much.

Hang on…

A scream

Something terrible has happened!

3pm

Dear Diary,

What a commotion!

Mrs Mirfield found out that Alice has been in the larder.

Mrs Mirfield had tried hiding the biscuit barrel, but Alice always finds it and steals the biscuits to share them with Ralph.

It is a bit naughty.

Mrs Mirfield went mad.

She shouted so loud I could hear from my bedroom.

Poor Alice! She must have felt so embarrassed. Rather than walk through the kitchen and get told off again, she snuck out into the garden through the back door.

Next thing there was a great big crash - then a pause - then the high screech of Mrs Mirfield screaming. We all rushed to the kitchen to see what was the matter. The way she was screaming we didn't dare think what had happened – had the Germans broken in? Had someone been killed?

I got to the larder first. It was a mess. It looked like a bomb had gone off!

The door was wide open, broken glass bottles, flour on the floor, long deep scratches all over the counter, and there in the middle was the biscuit barrel, smashed to pieces holding nothing but crumbs.

Mrs Mirfield's face had turned red, she was so angry. She stomped off into the garden shouting, "Alice! Come here!" and "Preposterous girl!" and I ended up stood all alone in the larder - alone… until Alfred the Butler came in.

He thought I'd made all the mess, stole the biscuits, smashed up the bottles and scratched the counter. I wanted to explain, that I'd been upstairs writing my diary, but he wouldn't let me speak.

He called me a horrible little girl. He told me that I didn't belong in Batley Hall. What a nasty, mean thing to say!

He sent me upstairs without any supper and gave me early bedtime for a week!

It was so unfair. I was so angry I screamed… into my pillow. I don't want Alfred to know he's upset me.

Anyway, now I've calmed down a bit, I'm going to read my Sherlock Holmes book.

4pm

Dear Diary,

The first Sherlock Holmes case is amazing – a case of a two burglars. They found a bookshop near a bank and every week they paid the bookseller to deliver his books to the other side of London. While the bookseller was out, the burglars tunneled up into the bank and stole all the money. Worst of all, when the bank found the tunnel, they thought the poor bookseller did it EVEN THOUGH HE WAS INNOCENT!

Soon, Sherlock was piecing together the clues…

HANG ON

… I could do this.

I'm innocent. I've been accused of a crime.

If I can just piece all the clues together, I'd crack the case just like Sherlock Holmes.

Let me see. What are the facts that I know?

ALICE

1. Earlier on, Alice went to the larder to steal biscuits.
2. She always finds biscuits and shares them with Ralph.

Hmm… it does seem like Alice is the prime suspect so far.

DOORS

1. There are 2 doors into the larder. One from the kitchen, one from the garden.
2. The door to the garden is usually locked.
3. When Mrs Mirfield shouted she left the larder through the back door.
4. Nobody entered the larder through the kitchen, because Mrs Mirfield would have seen them.
5. When I arrived in the larder the key was missing.

Of course… whoever broke the biscuit barrel must have come in through the garden door!

LARDER

1. There were things broken everywhere. The thief must be very messy.
2. There were scratch marks on the counter tops. You'd need something sharp to make scratches that big.
3. There was nothing left but crumbs – whoever the thief is, they eat super quickly. And they didn't mind eating things that fell on the floor.
4. The flour on the floor had some kind of animal foot prints in.

It's elementary! The criminal is RALPH!

RALPH

1. He hasn't got a knife, but he's got long sharp CLAWS.
2. He's messy, he wolfs down his food.
3. He's not fussy – he'd definitely eat something that had fallen on the floor
4. He watched Alice come out from the larder with a biscuit – therefore he knew where the biscuits were kept.
5. When he heard Mrs Mirfield open the door from the kitchen, he would have run out the back door like a shot.

I've done it I've cracked the case: Charlotte Holmes and the Mystery of the Broken Biscuit Barrel.

I must tell Sir Jeremy at once!

8pm

Dear Diary,

Hooray! What a success!

I explained to Sir Jeremy all of the clues and how they showed Ralph broke the biscuit barrel, not me.

He knew I was right.

He told me how proud I had made him – how clever I'd been.

Best of all he overruled Alfred – I got to eat dinner with double pudding too! And my bedtime is back to 8.30 again.

Alfred looked very sheepish. Sir Jeremy made him apologise to me. He looked like his head would explode. That was my best Yorkshire moment so far by a mile!

Poor Alice got a telling off for leaving the door open, and Mrs Mirfield's ordering a special biscuit box with a lock and a key. There'll be no biscuit scrumping any more.

Ralph's looking happy. Even though he's been naughty, I still gave him a great big stroke. And what did I find in his fur? Hundreds of CRUMBS! He really is a greedy animal.

I'm going to open my Sherlock Holmes book again. Just enough time to finish the chapter and then it will be time for bed.

I've got a feeling I've a lot more to learn from Sherlock Holmes before I can become a super detective.

4 WAR

Sunday 3rd September1939

Dear Diary,

This morning Sir Jeremy took me to church. Batley is such a pretty place and the vicar, Rev Kindly, is a very jolly sort of fellow. He smiled and waved when he saw me. He told me how delighted he was to have someone come and visit all the way from London.

Before we could finish the first hymn, the verger ran in and told everyone to be quiet. He turned up the radio and we heard the Prime Minister. He said Britain is going to war!

Everybody fell silent.

After a few moments, Rev Kindly stood up and said a short prayer. He prayed that everyone would be safe and that the war would be over quickly. We all said amen and we all really meant it.

Then the organist started playing and we all sang the hymn "Eternal Father." When we got to the line "Oh, hear us when we cry to Thee for those in peril on the sea!" Mrs Mirfield started crying and Henry held her hand very tightly.

When we got back I saw Henry and Mrs Mirfield in the kitchen. They were hugging each other and crying. I didn't go in.

Sir Jeremy said there wouldn't be any lunch, so I went to my room and read about Sherlock Holmes and the Adventure of the Musgrave Ritual. It was all about a butler and a maid who stole some priceless treasure and then disappeared. Sherlock worked out what had happened though. He was so clever.

As I hadn't had any lunch, by suppertime I was really hungry. I went down to find out what we were having for supper but I couldn't find anybody anywhere.

All the men of the house were in Sir Jeremy's study. They looked worried. I stood by the door and listened.

Johnson asked something about conscription. From what I could tell, the government said all the men had to join the army. He didn't look very pleased about it. He said he had people he didn't want to leave behind.

Sir Jeremy said he understood, but he didn't think conscription would affect Batley Hall. Alfred was too old, Doug had a limp and Johnson was an essential worker. Alfred said he didn't think drivers were essential workers, but Sir Jeremy told him "of course he's essential. I don't know how to drive. How do you expect me to get to my appointments? I shall write to the war office first thing in the morning." Johnson looked very relieved.

As they left the study I asked Sir Jeremy what Mrs Mirfield was making for supper. Sir Jeremy said Mrs Mirfield wasn't feeling very well and everyone had to make their own supper from what they could find in the larder. Alice and I had jam and crumpets and listened to King George on the radio.

The King said there were going to be dark times ahead.

Alice said I shouldn't be scared. That everything would turn out alright.

I'm not sure I believe her.

I hope Mum's not scared. I must write her a letter so she knows I'm alright...

5 BIRDS

Monday 4th September 1939

Dear Diary,

What a wonderful day I've had being outdoors: glorious sunshine, colourful flowers, merry birdsong. I wish I could live here in Yorkshire forever.

It's so different to London. Not many people have gardens where we live. There are trees, but they're mostly planted on the streets posh people live in. It's so nice to see so much green all around. After the war's finished, I'll bring Mum to Batley Hall. She'd love it here. It might make her happy. I'd give anything just to see her be happy.

Doug says that nature blesses all men alike. I met him today – he's Sir Jeremy's groundsman.

He looks after all of the plants, the trees and all of the wildlife at Batley Hall. It's a very big job for one man, and everything always looks lovely. I don't know how he has time to do it all.

He gave me a bird book with all kinds of birds in it. He pointed some out in the garden as well. He knows loads about birds.

He even taught me how to make a birdfeeder in the greenhouse. We used string, a tube, lard and some seeds. My hands were so messy – all covered in grease. Anyway, it worked pretty well. I've hung the bird feeder outside of my window so I can see from my bedroom what birds come to it.

Doug said, if I want, he'll teach me how to look after the plants.

He's such a nice man.

He said he'd noticed that Ralph had dug up his turnips - he laughed about it. He thought it was funny. He called Ralph "a terror", but you could tell that he didn't really mean it. He said "I don't blame him, it's in his nature. If I were a dog, I'd be digging up turnips as well."

It's silly, but I can really imagine Doug being a dog. Doug the dog… it almost rhymes. He's got muddy paws, he loves digging in the garden, and he's always friendly and he never gets cross. I think Doug would make a lovely dog just like Ralph.

Henry would be a puppy – he's so full of energy all the time.

Alice – she'd be a mole. She gets around all over the house without being seen.

Johnson wouldn't be a dog. He'd be a horse or a pony. He loves going fast in the car, so he'd probably love racing about in the meadow. He could use his car polish to polish his saddle.

Mrs Mirfield – she's more tricky. She'd be a badger. She does her own thing, and you don't want to mess with her. And she's got a streak of white in her hair – just like a badger has.

Alfred – He's a snake - one to be wary of. He even hisses when he speaks. Eeew, I really don't like snakes… then again, I don't really like Alfred.

Sir Jeremy – he's more a bear. He'd be a kindly old bear - one who shares pots of honey. He'd think lots and say little, but always be kind.

Mum would be an eagle. Strong, quick and nothing gets past her.

I must write her a letter. I always forget.

And me… what would I be… I wouldn't be an animal. I'd be a super detective. Just like Sherlock Holmes.

Sir Jeremy says that if I want to be a super detective I must be more observant. He says Sherlock never missed a clue – that's what made him so great.

Doug says nature's full of clues. He says living things have a lot they can teach us, as long as we learn to observe them.

I've been observing my birdfeeder now for an hour. So far I've only seen one bird. I didn't get a good look at it, but it had black and white feathers, so I think it was a magpie. The book says that magpies are common in Yorkshire, so I wouldn't be surprised if it were.

There are geese in the Sherlock Holmes story I'm reading. He's so clever; he's managed to prove that two geese bought by two different men are actually both the same goose. I don't know how that'll help crack the case yet, but I'm sure that it's going to be useful.

6 UP AND DOWN

Tuesday 5th September 1939

Dear Diary,

Today has been a very strange day:

- I failed at being a super detective AGAIN!
- I fell out with Henry.
- I missed most of breakfast.
- I got told off by Alfred.
- I upset Sir Jeremy.
- Two quite unexpected things happened.

Last night, I finished Sherlock Holmes and the Adventure of the Blue Carbuncle – the one about the two geese. I was sure I had pieced together all of the clues. Just like Sherlock Holmes was doing. I was feeling really proud of myself. Then in the end all my guesses were WRONG. I'm not sure I'm cut out to be a super detective at all.

I was still fed up when I woke up. I was still fed up when I went to breakfast. I was still fed up when I buttered my toast.

Henry asked me what was wrong. I told him, "I'm fed up. I'm not a detective and I'm not very super."

Henry told me he thought I was super, which was nice (I suppose), but he thinks everything's super. Yesterday, when we walked Ralph in the field he stood in a cow pat and thought that was super.

He said he was going to cheer me up whether I wanted him to or not.

Then, without warning, he snatched my toast out of my hand and started tearing it up into little bits.

How rude!

I didn't complain; I was too fed up. Besides, I was so fed up I wasn't enjoying my toast anyway.

Next, he grabbed all the spoons he could find and lined them up on the edge of the table. Into each spoon he placed a little torn off square of toast.

"Watch this," he said and then "FIRE!" He walloped the handle of one the spoons and sent the toast flying right up in the air. It nearly hit the ceiling!

"Careful! That toast nearly hit the ceiling," I said.

He said, "I know. Isn't that funny?" then "stand clear" then "FIRE!" then he fired spoon-cannon two.

I told him not to aim at the ceiling. Henry asked, "What should

I aim at?" And then it got silly.

Before very long there was toast in the fish bowl. Toast on the window. Toast in the fireplace. He lit the three candles in the candle stand and shot bits of toast at them to make them go out. It was pretty impressive. Henry's always good at that kind of thing.

It knew it was naughty, but I suppose it must have cheered me up a little bit. When he ran out of toast he shouted, "SUPPLIES!" so I tore up some bacon and took it over.

Henry said, "Thank you, Lieutenant Gunner. RELOAD!"

And that's how he got me involved.

It got very messy.

The grease made the bacon bits stick to the wall.

"We've run out of bacon," I told him.

"Very well, Lieutenant," Henry replied. "Prepare to load heavy mortar shell."

I grabbed a soft boiled egg from the bowl and balanced it on the spoon.

Henry put his fingers in his ears and said, "You fire this one, Lieutenant."

I shouted, "FIRE IN THE HOLE!" Hit the spoon and fired my very first volley into the air.

The egg went up.

The dining room door opened.

The egg went up.

Alfred entered the room.

The egg seemed to hang in the air like a feather.

Alfred looked at the mess and he looked very cross.

The egg started falling.

"What on Earth do you brats think you're doing?" Alfred yelled at the top of his voice.

I didn't know what to answer. So I just answered "Egg."

"Egg? What does that mean?" Alfred asked.

We both yelled, "Egg!"

Henry pointed and shouted, "Take cover!"

Alfred looked up just in time to see the soft boiled egg fall the final four inches onto his face and explode.

It was everywhere.

Yoke in his eyes, in his hair, in his ears.

I've never seen him so angry. He advanced double time and rolled up his sleeves.

Quick as a fox Henry opened the window and climbed to outside and to safety.

Before I could follow, Alfred had grabbed me.

Oh, what a telling off I got. I was marched to Sir Jeremy's study. Sir Jeremy gave me a lecture on how disappointed he was… I could have died of embarrassment.

Of course, I was given punishment chores. I had to clean up the dining room and wash up the breakfast pots and pans in the kitchen.

All on my own too! All because Henry was too scared to come back in the house.

Oh, that makes me so mad!
I'm going to really fall out with him about this.

After I cleaned up the mess, I collected up leftovers and took them to the larder, whistling the tune that Johnson taught me to keep up my morale.

As I was whistling through the kitchen, a voice shouted out from the larder.

"I can hear you! Hurry up! I've been waiting. I've got a surprise for you!"

I thought it was strange – who'd be waiting for me? But I do like surprises, so I sped up a bit.

I walked in and saw Alice the maid, stood on the countertop, dusting the jars on the very top shelf. She didn't look down at me.

"Sorry, I'm just in the middle of dusting. What's this?" She picked up a package from off the top shelf. "Sweets for a sweetheart… it's a present for you!" And with that she spun round, chocolates in hand and froze when she saw me by the door.

Can you believe it? A box of chocolates just for me! And when chocolate is rationed because of the war! I thanked her and thanked her and thanked her again.

But - Alice seemed a little uncomfortable. She made me promise not to tell Alfred, then put down the box and rushed out.

I opened the chocolates and closed the door so I could enjoy them in secret.

I had a fudge roll and a hazelnut whirl and had just popped in a strawberry crème when I heard someone in the kitchen whistling a familiar tune.

Next came a knock on the larder door.

A voice called out. It was Johnson's. "Sorry I'm late. I've come to cheer you up. I brought you a present. Something lovely for somebody lovely." He burst through the door holding a big bunch of flowers.

Strange – when he saw me he froze, just like Alice had frozen.

Another present! For me! Fresh from the gardens.

I thanked him and took them out of his hand.

"Would you like a chocolate?" I asked him "They're scrummy. Alice just gave them to me!"

"Alice was here?" he asked.

"Yes. You just missed her. She went out the back door."

"Oh right." Johnson said. "Well, best be off." And with that he left out the back.

What lovely people. What wonderful presents.

Well, if there's one thing I've learned today, it is expect the unexpected.

One minute life gives you lectures and chores, the next it's all chocolates and flowers!

I do hope somebody gives them lovely presents.

7 HIT THE DECK

Wednesday 6ᵗʰ September 1939

Dear Diary,

It's raining.

It's been raining all day.

I spent all morning by myself. Sir Jeremy gave me an old deck of cards from his bureau. He taught me how to play patience, a game you can play on your own.

I played it all morning. I felt ever so lonely.

After lunch, Henry came round to apologise for what happened yesterday. His mum told him off for leaving me to take all the blame. She's made him do washing up for the rest of the week. I think that sounds fair.

Anyway, I forgave him. I do like him lots, and he's not a bad person. Everybody can make a mistake. Besides there isn't really anyone else here to play with.

I showed him my flowers and shared out my chocolates. He asked me where I had got them, but I wouldn't say. I kept it all secret. Secret chocolates taste better than normal ones.

Henry taught me a new game called Beggar My Neighbour. It's really fun, and we're much better matched than at mikado. I won four games, Henry only won three.

Now I'm going to read the next chapter in my Sherlock Holmes book.

I'm reading *Sherlock Holmes and the Field Bazaar*. It's about a letter sent by an unknown person. Sherlock Holmes has to figure out who wrote it. I've had a guess, but I'm probably wrong.

I must write that letter to Mum…

8 SEARCHING FOR ANSWERS

Friday 8th September 1939

11am

Dear Diary,

Disaster!

I've lost my notes on the Sherlock Holmes mysteries. I've been making notes on them while I'm sat down in the drawing room. They're just little jottings - the things I've been thinking. I never imagined anyone else would read them. But last night I left them downstairs by accident.

This morning I got up early and went down to fetch them. I looked and I looked, but I just couldn't find them.

I asked Alfred. He said he hadn't seen them and that if he had, he would have thrown them away. He said if somebody has picked them up, it'll be Alice. Alfred said she's often the first to get up, so if I had to go pestering, to go pester her.

Well I looked, and I looked and I couldn't find Alice: not in the larder, not in the bedrooms, not in the kitchen, the dining room, patio, not in the garden, the greenhouse, the meadow... I even looked all round the under stairs cupboard.

The notes, then the maid – both seemed to have vanished. It was all very strange indeed.

People don't disappear. Not without leaving clues. Sherlock would find her. I just had to be methodical.

I asked Mrs Mirfield. She didn't know.

I asked Henry and Doug, but they both shook their heads... very peculiar.

Next try was Johnson. I went to the garage.

I've not had a reason to go there before – whenever there's been any driving to be done, Johnson just brings the car round to the front.

The doors of the garage are huge and wooden. The closer I got to them, the bigger they seemed to become. By the time I was standing next to them I felt very tiny indeed.

*　　*　　*　　*　　*

I knocked. Nobody answered.

I called out, "Hello?" and "Johnson?", but got no reply.

Gingerly I pushed on the door.

It opened with a loud creak, and a blast of a song being played on a gramophone. The same tune that Johnson had taught me.

"Hello?" I called.

I listened and heard someone laughing.

I called again: "Johnson?" And stepped inside the building.

There wasn't much light in the garage, and what little there was, was broken up into patches by the ivy growing over the windows.

The music was louder inside, as was the laughing. Despite all the gloom and stale air, it sounded quite fun.

Laughter. A low voice. I knew it was Johnson. Then…

Laughter – Eureka! That's Alice. I've finally found her!

I walked towards where the din was all coming from, shouting out: "Alice? Johnson? I'm coming to find you"

I must have been heard, because someone turned down the music.

"Alice, are you there? It's me. It's Charlotte. I've been looking for you all morning."

"Charlotte!" cried Alice.

"Charlotte! Come in. Why don't I get some more light?" Johnson said, and then whoosh, he threw open two large shutters and light flooded in through the whole of the garage.

*   *   *   *   *

Alice was sat on the running board of Sir Jeremy's car, with a picnic, (wine glasses, blanket, candles and all) laid out on top of the bonnet. If it had been in a park, you might call it romantic.

As soon as she saw me she jumped to her feet. "What a surprise. I didn't expect to see your face here, Charlotte. What brings you down here?"

"I came to find Johnson, to help me find you," I said.

"Well here we all are!" Johnson said. "You can stop looking."

I was so very intrigued by the in-the-dark car picnic, for a moment I forgot all about my lost notes. "What are you doing in here?" I asked. "Are you being romantic?"

They looked at each other. Then Alice explained.

> *First of all, no. It wasn't romantic. Alfred's rules were very clear: staff romances were strictly banned. Neither of them would risk their jobs for a silly secret romantic picnic. The truth of matter, said Alice was that at 10:30 she'd come down to dust Sir Jeremy's car, not knowing Johnson was going to be there.*

> *Two minutes later, by chance, Johnson had come back to the garage to pick up his gloves which he'd left on the side. So when they bumped into each other, they got chatting, then started to feel faint and suddenly both of them realised they accidentally hadn't had breakfast that morning.*

> *They didn't want to bother Mrs Mirfield for food, and Johnson remembered he kept an emergency picnic, with wine glasses, a table cloth and candles locked in his cabinet. They didn't have a*

table, so they laid it out on the car.

When they sat down, the bright sunlight had made Alice sneeze, so they closed the shutters and lit the small candles. As for the music, Johnson had by chance borrowed some records from a friend the night before. They didn't know quite how Sir Jeremy's gramophone had ended up in the garage and intended to return it as soon as they could.

Still as it was there, they decided to put on the records just for a bit of fun.

Not that they had any fun. In fact, both of them said they had no fun at all, which meant Alfred did not need to know. In fact, they were very clear on that point – It was nothing romantic, it all happened by chance and Alfred should not be told anything.

Of course I agreed. It all sounded perfectly reasonable, and a little bit funny. Fancy all those things happening by chance. What a strange combination of coincidences!

*   *   *   *   *

Once they were convinced that I wouldn't tell Alfred, Alice asked what I had come in there looking for. I told her: "My papers that I left in the drawing room. A pile of them, covered in scribbles and notes."

"Oh, those were yours were they?" Alice replied "I did pick them up. But I thought they were Sir Jeremy's. I put them into his study and locked the door. Were they important? What did they say?"

"Private thoughts," I explained.

"I'm sorry, Charlotte. I just didn't know. Perhaps if you go to Sir Jeremy's office. Maybe he's not had a chance to read over them. Perhaps you could just ask for them back."

I knew she was right. I had to be quick. I turned on my heels and made my way back.

Behind me I heard Johnson turn the gramophone back up, followed by a couple of giggles. As I neared the exit, the shutters reshuttered and twilight resumed.

$$*\qquad*\qquad*\qquad*\qquad*$$

I walked double quick – it still took me 5 minutes to get to the main Hall. I bolted up the front door steps and into the broad high chest of Alfred.

He sneered and reminded me house rules are strictly no running. He pronounced the word strictly particularly clearly. Without pause, he continued: "I hoped I'd bump into you. Sir Jeremy's mentioned you. He said something came across his desk this morning that's made him very concerned. He'd like to converse with you on the matter. He's reading it again now and reflecting upon it. Report to his office at 11.30 sharp."

Stones in my stomach.

Alfred continued, "and wash your face, child. You've got black marks all over you. Anyone would think you've been working in a car garage. There are such things as standards, you know."

Well. That's everything there is to know. It's nearly 11.30 now. I better go speak to Sir Jeremy. Oh, I do hope that everything turns out OK...

12pm

Dear Diary,

It's over! I've talked to Sir Jeremy. He read everything, every word, every note in the margin. He knows my thoughts better than I do.

He read them out. All of them. So I could hear them out loud.

"I've read 10 of the stories: I haven't guessed a single ending right"

"I'm not determined enough to be a super detective."

"If I was open-minded, you'd see my brain was empty..."

"If I was at all logical I'd have given up trying"

"I've been trying as hard as I can – it just isn't good enough. Who am I pretending to be? Who am I pretending this for? Nobody cares. I don't care... about me. I feel really rubbish."

"I wish I had just one reason to feel proud of myself, but there isn't one. Everything I do is rubbish. It's all a load of rubbish."

"Sherlock is the real Holmes, Charlotte's a fake. I wish Dad had been called something more normal. I should be called Charlotte Everyman... or Charlotte Unspecial."

There were so many comments! On and on. 2 pages, 3 pages, 4 pages... 5 minutes, 10 minutes... it felt like it lasted 10 hours.

Then it stopped. And then it was just me. Everything was out in the open. There was nowhere I could hide.

Sir Jeremy said he was concerned. That he feels sorry for me and that he wishes I didn't feel so sad. He told me I mustn't doubt myself. That none of the things I had written were true.

He reminded me about how I solved The Mystery of the Broken Biscuit Barrel. He told me that proves that I'm logical, open minded and determined, just like Sherlock Holmes.

He told me I mustn't be too hard on myself. He said Sherlock

Holmes had been a detective for 20 years before he solved the cases in the book. He said that as long as I practice I'll be every bit as good as Sherlock Holmes ever was.

He told me I mustn't think that nobody cares about me because they do. He told me that everybody here at Batley Hall cares about me: Henry, Alice, Mrs Mirfield, Doug, Ralph and even Alfred (though he has a funny way of showing it).

He said he was very proud of me, and if Mum knew how good I had been, she would be proud of me too.

Then we rang Mum.

$$* \quad * \quad * \quad * \quad *$$

She cried when she heard my voice. It was so nice to talk to her.

I told her I'm sorry I didn't write yet. I promised her I'd write soon. I've got so much to tell her about. About Sherlock Holmes, reading the books, and how I'm going to be a super detective.

Then after a short pause, she spoke.

She told me there was another side to my dad

When dad died, she vowed to put the past behind them

If I want to be a detective, I have their backing

She told me…

…I've always had the truth just in case.

Then she said she wouldn't say any more. If I was serious, that was enough.

But what did she mean?

What is the truth? She says that I've always had it *just in case.*

What does that mean? Just in case what?

But what if it's not? What if it's…

- just -

- in -

- case -

JUST IN MY SUITCASE!

12:15pm

Dear Diary,

I found it!

The photo mum taped in the lid of my box! It's a photo of her and Dad.

Those things that she told me: there was **another side** to my father, the past is **behind them**, I have their **backing**. She was telling me I have to look on the back of the photo. I peeled it off carefully, and on the back was a diagram that looked like this:

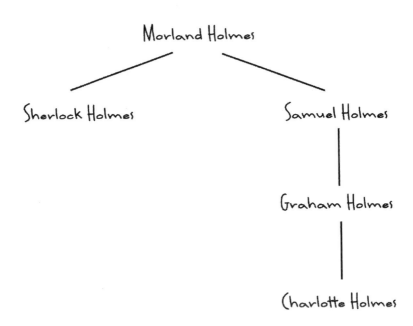

Is this true? Was my dad Sherlock's Nephew?

Am I related to Sherlock Holmes?

All of this time I was doubting myself. Now it turns out I'm as Holmes as it gets!

Thank you, Sir Jeremy. Thanks, Mum. I promise I'll never give up on myself again. I'll make you all proud of me. That's a guarantee!

9 A NEW LEAF

Saturday 9th September 1939

Saturday 9th September 1939

10am

Dear Diary,

Today is a wonderful day. When I woke up, I felt like a dark cloud had lifted. This is the start of a new improved story: "Charlotte Holmes turns a new leaf."

Henry, Ralph and I went for an extra long walk first thing in the morning. We spotted two new birds: a kittiwake and a blue tit. Henry said he thought he saw an ostrich – but I'm not sure they have any ostriches in Yorkshire.

When we got back I helped Mrs Mirfield with breakfast and washed up without being asked.

I even saw Alfred in the ballroom. He gave me a letter that came in the post. I was ever so polite to him. All please and thank you very much. Then I told him I thought he looked handsome in his waistcoat today. He didn't know quite what to say to that. He just blushed and walked away muttering.

I'm going to open it now.

Dear Charlotte,

I never told you much about your father. Whenever you asked me about his side of the family, I said I didn't know. But that wasn't the truth.

Forgive me. I have kept a secret from you for so long, but now you know who you truly are. It is true: your father's uncle was Sherlock Holmes.

The whole Holmes family are master detectives. They have a gift. Your father wanted to follow in his uncle's footsteps, solving crimes and uncovering the truth. Just like his Uncle Sherlock, there was no case he couldn't crack — every bad guy knew it. And every bad guy wanted to stop him. I begged him to stop before he upset someone dangerous, but he wouldn't listen. He told me "no bad guy will ever kill Graham Holmes" — he was wrong.

I should have told you earlier, but I just couldn't bear the thought of the same thing happening to you. I knew you were bound to figure it out sooner or later — you are a Holmes after all.

If you're reading this, you're every bit the detective your father was, and Sherlock Holmes before him. There won't be a case you can't crack. Just be careful it doesn't crack you.

I love you Charlotte.

Stay safe

Your very proud Mum

P.S. I believe in you, Charlotte. Now believe in yourself.

7pm

Dear Diary,

Doug's been teaching me and Henry about trees this afternoon.

There are so many types of trees, all with different names, different bark, different sizes and leaves. It's going to take some effort to remember them all.

He let me have his poster of tree leaves. I've clipped it up on the wall with a bulldog clip, so it's easy to take down if I want to go to the park with it.

Doug told us an ancient saying: "A society grows great when old men plant trees in whose shade they know they shall never sit."

Some of the trees here are hundreds of years old. It's incredible when you think about it.

My favourite tree at Batley Hall is the sycamore tree. It's ever so tall, and so wide round the trunk. It feels almost magical. I can't wait for the helicopter seeds to start falling.

Henry's favourite's the horse chestnut tree because of the conkers. He said he's been the best conkerer at his school for 5 years straight. He says the trick is to soak them in vinegar then they go really hard like rocks and they smash everyone else's to pieces.

Doug had an idea we could collect different leaves and make them into pieces of art. Henry and I think it's a great idea. We both love art and we both love climbing trees, so it's perfect.

We've already collected loads of different leaves from the grounds. The only leaves we couldn't find were oak leaves.

Doug says it's probably a good thing that there aren't too many oak trees at Batley Hall. Oak leaves and acorns are poisonous to dogs and it would be terrible if Ralph accidentally ate some and got sick.

Still, our collages would look really good with some oak leaves on...

Down in the drawing room, I found a book called "Notable Trees of West Yorkshire." It says a disease came and killed off the oak trees, and now there are no oaks for miles and miles. That is, except one. And it's in Alfred's garden.

Henry and I have a plan. We're going to sneak in at night and while Alfred's asleep collect some leaves and no-one will know we were there.

I've not been to Alfred's house before, but Henry has… once. He says it takes an hour to walk there. It's not on a road, so you have to navigate by using the hills and landmarks. He says that it's easy as long as it's not foggy.

Apparently the garden has a wall around it – a really high wall. Alfred is so paranoid about anybody getting anywhere near his oak tree that he'd rather see nothing but walls through his windows than have even the chance that someone might sneak in.

Henry says it's much too high for one person to climb over it alone, but with two of us, he thinks we'll be able to boost our way over the top.

It's going to be so fun. We're going tonight!

Once everyone's fallen asleep, Henry's going to throw stones at my window, and then we'll sneak out. An hour walk there, ten minutes picking leaves, an hour walk back - we'll be back in bed before anybody knows that we're gone.

Henry says he's going to sneak the key for the biscuit box, so we can take biscuits to keep us going.

I've already borrowed an old pair of wellies from Doug, and Johnson has lent me his torch. I didn't say what it was for, of course. Still, he was happy to help

10 ALFRED'S SECRET GARDEN

Sunday 10th September 1939

Dear Diary,

We did it. We made it… alive.

I NEVER WANT TO GO BACK TO ALFRED'S GARDEN FOR AS LONG AS I LIVE!

It started off fine. Henry came to my window. He didn't need to throw any stones. I was far too excited to be asleep anyway.

When I heard his feet on the gravel I threw my bag out the window and he helped me climb down the balcony to the ground.

Henry had come well prepared. As well as his cagoule and a handful of biscuits he had:

- a rope for climbing.
- scissors for leaf-cutting.
- spare socks in case he stepped a puddle.
- a box of matches for fire-lighting.
- and his mum's rolling pin for "bonking anyone over the head with."

Quite who he imagined we'd need to bonk over the head I don't really know – but it was there as a last resort.

The night was quite cool and a little bit moist. There were wisps of fog and a nice big bright moon. As we walked down the drive and off the estate, we looked up and could make out a face in the moon. Henry thinks one day mankind will visit the moon. I don't know. It sounds crazy to me. We haven't even worked out how to live next to each other without going to war. Imagine how much harder flying to the moon would be.

$$* \quad * \quad * \quad * \quad *$$

The walk to Alfred's took much longer that we thought it would. For a start it took us 15 minutes just to get off Sir Jeremy's estate! Then it was another 20 minutes until we had walked though and out of Batley proper (Alfred's house was on the opposite side of the town).

We wondered how often Alfred did this walk home. Of course most nights he stays in his room at Batley Hall, and Henry remembered Johnson giving him a lift on occasion. But I can't imagine him walking it on ANY day. It's so far and Alfred isn't very fit.

By 30 minutes in we had eaten the biscuits and sung all the songs Henry knew from his scout camp. The cold tendrils of night started to worm their way into our shoes; toes started to numb. We put our cagoules on.

Henry said he didn't think Alfred should get to own a tree if he built a wall round it so no one could see it. He said Doug told him trees belong to the Earth and not people. I think I agree. How can you own something that was alive for 400 years before you were born? If anything – trees should own us.

*   *   *   *   *

It was dark on the paths. The government's special wartime blackout law mean that all of the street lamps have been taken out, houses have to have solid black curtains and cars have special covers on their headlamps so they only let out tiny slivers of light.

It's for a good reason. It's so German planes can't see where the towns are which makes them more difficult to bomb. I thought about Mum, on her own, in London. That is the first place the Germans will go for. It is big and much, much closer to France. Yorkshire is much safer by comparison. German planes can barely reach us up here. And who'd want to drop bombs on Batley anyway?

It was naughty for us to bring torches out with us. You can get yourself into a lot of trouble shining lights at night. We swore not to use them except in emergencies, which was fine because the big moon was like one massive torch and we could see plenty with that.

*   *   *   *   *

As we got further on out into the countryside the fog started building. Clouds moved in over the bright shining moon and we found ourselves losing our bearings and having to backtrack to get on the right path. It felt different to how it felt when we set out. It felt creepy, dangerous, intimidating.

Fortunately, after a third bit of backtracking, it wasn't too long before Henry could point out Alfred's house on the hill.

It sat all on its own as if it had no friends. Maybe it didn't have any friends. If somebody's house was going to have no friends, it would certainly be Alfred's.

Of course it made sense. Alfred would hate having neighbours: talking over the fence, borrowing garden shears, asking how their mothers were and listening to them sing carols at Christmas. I can't imagine Alfred doing any of those things. No wonder he wanted to live on his own.

His house was well kept, but incredibly plain looking. He had no flowers, no hanging baskets. His brickwork had no ornamentation – nothing. The walls went up and down and were flat. They met in a corner, were square and exact.

It was soulless – the kind of place an accountant would live in, and not ever laugh in - the kind of house that never has a Christmas tree or crackers.

One thing it wasn't was scary.

I sort of felt sorry for Alfred. The most exciting part of his life was his job, and he hates everyone at Batley Hall except Sir Jeremy. If it wasn't for getting to boss people around what would his life really be? I thought, "when I get back I might let him boss me around a bit more… as a treat for him."

*   *   *   *   *

The wall around the garden at the back was gigantic. Not so tall that the giant oak didn't peek over the top, but the closer you got the less tree you could see. It was as tall as me, Henry and half a Henry more. There was no way we were going to boost over that.

Henry looked round and found two sturdy branches and dug one end of each into the ground quite close to the wall. When they were leant against the wall they made a sort of slope you could climb. You had to be careful, one inch left or right and they slid down the wall, but after a few goes I was stood at the top, two or three feet off the ground.

Once I was steady, Henry did a run-up straight at the wall. At the last moment I grabbed his ankles and pushed. I pushed really hard, but as Henry went up, the branches slid down. Somehow he managed to hook all his fingers on top of the wall.

"Got it, I've got it," he said. "But I'm slipping."

I had to think quickly. I grabbed one of the branches and used it to push him up just a bit more. I pushed him right on the bum cheek. "Ow!" he yelled. "Can't you push something else?"

I said I couldn't. Of course, I could have, but it's a lot of fun poking a friend on the bum cheeks with a giant tree branch – you should make the most of the opportunity when it arises.

One final shove and suddenly Henry had enough of a grip to pull himself up. He lay on top of the wall.

"Wow!" he said. "This oak tree is enormous. You won't believe it!"

I threw him his bag. Henry tied off his rope on a nearby branch then let out the other end down to the ground. I grabbed the end of the rope and, with Henry holding onto the other end, started to climb.

Today I learned climbing a rope up a high, straight brick wall is really hard.

*   *   *   *   *

When I got to the top we both sat on the wall and looked down into the walled garden. It was a long drop, a VERY long drop.

From on top of the wall you could see everything. The back of Alfred's house was as dull as the front. Instead of garden furniture he had a single upturned orange crate – he clearly never had guests. There were no flowers, no colour. What a waste! My mum would kill to have a garden like this. Alfred didn't know how lucky he was.

Next to the orange crate stood a battered old scarecrow. It was dressed as a butler. Henry thought they must have been Alfred's old clothes.

He pointed out: "A scarecrow's so Alfred… he's not growing food. He's just put it up because he doesn't like birds. He's so mean he doesn't even want birds in his garden"

The star of the garden was the giant oak tree. It was broad, tall and laden with branches that bristled with leaves.

"Look," I said pointing to one of the nearby branches. "We can get all the leaves we want from up here. We don't even have to go into the garden."

"We could," said Henry. "But then we wouldn't have broken into Alfred's garden, would we? Surely we didn't come all this way to not break into Alfred's garden. Come on." We shuffled along the top of the wall to the oak branch where Henry had tied off the rope.

It didn't look safe.

Henry said it was ladies first. Good job I was feeling brave. Besides, with Henry at the top he could hold onto the branch so it didn't bend as much. Going second would be a much riskier descent.

I made it down quickly and without any scary moments. Henry threw down his bag and then prepared himself to follow. He leant back on the rope, but even before he put all his weight on it you could see the branch bending much more than before.

I whispered up loudly "I don't like the way that branch looks, Henry."

"Then I'll just have to not look at it," Henry replied, before closing his eyes and jumping off backwards.

*　　　*　　　*　　　*　　　*

He hit the ground hard... followed immediately by the branch.

*　　　*　　　*　　　*　　　*

It must have really hurt him. It made an almighty THWACK! Henry said he was OK, but his voice was all funny – so I think he was probably winded. Thank goodness the branch only broke when he was half-way down. If it had broken at the top, he might have broken his ankle.

A chink of light peeped round one of Alfred's upstairs blackout curtains.

"Quick, Alfred's heard us," I said as I helped Henry up, grabbing his bag and the rope and ducking round the far side of the tree. I counted to ten in my head and I snuck a peak back at the window. Alfred was stood at the window, investigating the noise. Next time I checked he had gone back to bed.

We'd made it. We'd broken inside Alfred's garden!

We merrily got to work snipping off leaves, tips of branches and even a few acorns.

After ten minutes or so, our thoughts turned to how we were going to get out.

The branch had broken so we couldn't go back up the rope.

"I've got an idea," I said. "The orange crate - I'll stand on that and give you a boost. It'll be easy."

We crept over to the house, picked up the crate and carried it over to the wall. I stood on it, Henry jumped and I grabbed hold of his ankles and pushed. But as Henry went up I was pushed down.

CRACK! The top of the orange crate split and I felt my feet land on the ground underneath.

"I've got it," said Henry as he hauled himself up. "Throw me my bag." I chucked it up after him.

Out of the corner of my eye I noticed the light switch on in Alfred's bedroom.

*   *   *   *   *

"Henry, I'm in trouble," I said. I was up to my waist in broken crate and could feel a few splinters in my legs.

"Throw me the rope!" Henry shouted back.

But I couldn't. I couldn't push myself free from the broken

orange crate.

I heard Alfred's heavy footsteps trampling down his staircase.

"Henry," I whined. "I'm stuck!"

The second thing I learned last night is Henry's the perfect friend to have in a crisis.

Without getting flustered he told me what to do.

I rocked myself sideways and onto the floor and wriggled myself free through the bottom of the crate. No sooner had I managed to get out, Alfred opened the door in his dressing gown all the time shouting and putting shoes on very angrily. He was calling us vandals and trespassers and some words I'd not heard before. He said he would catch us and call the police.

At least in the shadows he hadn't recognised us.

I grabbed the rope, but by then, Alfred had his shoes on and was charging towards me. I threw it to Henry, but it didn't go high enough. I've never been good at throwing things. I tried once again. It was lower than the first time! Henry said "One more go," but there just wasn't time. I dropped the rope just in time to dodge under Alfred's capturing arms and get myself round the far side of the tree. Henry yelled "Run for it." But I didn't need telling.

I felt my way around the tree. My heart was racing. It was so very dark. I could hear Alfred grunting and scratching around. He shouted "Who are you? I'll catch you, you know."

*　　　*　　　*　　　*　　　*

Suddenly a beam of light shone on the back door. It was Henry's torch! I started running.

I could hear Alfred chasing me. I was quicker than him, and I had a head start, so I easily got inside the house first. I ploughed headlong into the dark unfamiliar rooms.

I'd seen the house from all angles, so I had a good guess where the front door would be and got there with barely a misstep between. I put out my hand for the lock.

Oh no!

There wasn't one lock but many: three, maybe four. I started undoing catches.

I could hear Alfred coming through the house behind me. My fingers were nimble. The catches sprang open. Alfred turned round the corner as I turned all the deadlocks and before he could finish saying "you'll pay for it now" I pulled the door handle and…

It didn't open.

Bolts! There were bolts - bottom and top. I jumped to the top one, and slid it right over. Alfred lunged at me. I landed and ducked straight down. I felt Alfred's big arms brush against my hair.

I slid back the second bolt, grabbed the handle and pulled. Fresh air! Freedom! Escape!

And that's when I felt the hard slam of Alfred's giant hand on my shoulder.

"Not so fast," he said. "Now, let's see who we've got here."

He spun me around to face him.

"Aaagh!" he screamed. Closing his eyes and waving his hands up in the air.

Brilliant! Henry was stood in the door with his torch, pointing it straight into Alfred's eyes.

"You're blinding me," Alfred wailed as he flailed around helplessly.

Henry grabbed my hand, and we just started running.

*   *   *   *   *

I have never run faster or longer or further or in colder or darker conditions than I did last night. But thanks to Henry's quick-thinking and illegal torch-shining, we made it back home safe and sound and anonymous.

I passed out like a light switch and slept like a log, clutching a bag full of the rarest oak leaves and dreams full of leaf collages.

11 THE AFTERMATH

Monday 11th September 1939

Dear Diary,

Alfred didn't come in this morning. Sir Jeremy said he'd been attacked by burglars in the middle of the night. Apparently he actually caught one too, but they escaped after blinding him with an illegal torch. Constable Brighouse, Batley's policeman, went round and took a statement but, when Alfred couldn't give a description, he told him there was nothing he could do.

I made all the right noises: "Oh dear!" "Good golly!" "Is he alright?"

Sir Jeremy kindly gave him the afternoon off to go home and add a few rows of bricks to his wall.

I spent the afternoon making a sketch of Alfred being blinded by burglars. I'm really pleased with it. Now to add leaves to make it a leaf montage. I'm going to make Alfred out of oak leaves.

12 THE MYSTERY OF THE MISSING RING

Wednesday 13th September 1939

11am

Dear Diary,

What a morning I've just had... there has been a robbery at Batley Hall!

Sir Jeremy put me in charge of the investigation.

This morning, Sir Jeremy woke up to find that his signet ring (a family heirloom) was stolen while he was sleeping.

After what happened at Alfred's house, everyone's very on edge about burglars. Sir Jeremy's very upset, and confused. I spent all day interviewing the suspects. Here are the facts as I have found them.

SIR JEREMY

1. Went to bed at 10pm.
2. Opened the window to let in some air.
3. Locked the door.
4. Took off his ring and placed it on his bed side table.
5. Ralph the dog sleeps in the room with him.
6. Ralph barks at anyone (except Alice and/or anyone who gives him a biscuit).
7. When he woke up, the ring was missing.
8. He called out for help. First Doug appeared at the window, shortly followed by Alfred who unlocked his door.
9. The only clue left behind was a black and white feather.

ALFRED

1. Locked up the whole house last night at 10.30pm.
2. Ralph barked at him as he went to bed. He doesn't like Ralph.
3. He slept through the night, didn't hear any disturbance.
4. He does have a skeleton key which opens up every door in the building.
5. When he heard Sir Jeremy cry, he rushed straight in.
6. Off the record, he doesn't trust Doug. But then, I don't think Alfred really trusts anybody.

JOHNSON

1. Says he wasn't at Batley Hall last night between 10.30pm-2am.
2. Refuses to reveal where he was last night.
3. Confessed that he "borrowed" Sir Jeremy's car last night WITHOUT Sir Jeremy's permission.
4. He was spotted outside the house flashing his lights about 10.30pm.
5. Henry woke up and marked down the sequence of flashes.
6. The flashes spell ALICE NOW in Morse code.
7. He has left a catalogue of expensive rings in the glove box of Sir Jeremy's car.

MRS MIRFIELD

1. Stayed up late baking cakes (went to bed at midnight).
2. Claims that she didn't hear anyone moving around downstairs.
3. She doesn't trust Alice. She's got her marked as a thief.
4. She doesn't wear jewellery because it interferes with her cooking.

HENRY

1. Went to bed early (around 8.00pm).
2. Was woken by flashing lights.
3. Is good at breaking into places (e.g. you know where).

ALICE

1. She claims she was not at Batley Hall last night between 10.30pm-2am.
2. She refuses to say where she was last night.
3. She has a skeleton key in the cleaning cupboard.
4. She uses it regularly to go in and out of other people's rooms.
5. Ralph never barks at her, he even knows her scent.
6. She has a black and white feather duster.
7. She's often told Sir Jeremy how much she loves that ring, and how she wished she could have one like it.

DOUG

1. Was up late picking slugs off his lettuces (till 12pm).
2. Claims he didn't hear anything unusual outside.
3. Has been trimming the ivy round Batley Hall for a week.
4. He uses big ladders which can easily reach to the upper floor windows.
5. He doesn't think anybody on the staff would steal something like that.
6. He thinks Sir Jeremy's probably lost it.

I'm pretty sure I can rule Mrs Mirfield out. She didn't give me any impression she could or they would do anything like this.

I know Henry is good at breaking into places, but why would he break in to Sir Jeremy's room? It just makes no sense. I don't think it's him.

Johnson – he's a bit more suspicious. Why all the big secrets? And there was that catalogue of valuable rings… if he loves valuable rings he might REALLY love Sir Jeremy's signet ring – it's beautiful. Still, I don't see how he could have done it *even if* he wanted to. He doesn't have a key or a ladder long enough to get in through Sir Jeremy's window. Besides which, by all accounts he was only here for 5 minutes, flashed a few lights and then left. Sir Jeremy's cross that he took the car without asking – but it's a big jump from borrowing a car without asking to breaking in and burgling! No, whatever Johnson was up to last night, he wasn't stealing the ring. He is innocent.

What about Alfred? He does have the key, but the dog really hates him. He barks any time Alfred even goes near him. He barks when Alfred walks along the corridor outside. I don't see how he could have done anything without Ralph waking everyone up. He can't even distract him with biscuits, not since Mrs Mirfield's got them under lock and key. No, Alfred is innocent.

So who is left, I'm choosing between Doug and Alice. Hmm. Both seem possible. She has a key. He has the big ladders.

Alfred suspected Doug did it, on the other hand, Mrs Mirfield said Alice. Doug is so lovely, I can't imagine him burgling anything – maybe that's his big secret. And he says he was working late, but nobody saw him. There's no way to check if he's lying or not.

If it's not Doug, that only leaves Alice. Oh Alice! Where did she get to last night? She won't say! We know she loves Sir Jeremy's signet ring and she could never afford to buy one herself. And she's got a track record of stealing the biscuits from Mrs Mirfield's larder.

And then there were those flashing lights that Henry saw: ALICE NOW. What was that all about? Could it have been a signal? Could it have meant "ALICE, NOW it's time to steal Sir Jeremy's ring?" Something doesn't make sense. There must be some kind of clue I'm missing.

The black and white feather in Sir Jeremy's room… it wasn't there when he went to bed. Whoever stole the ring must have left it behind. Now where have I seen a feather like that before?

I've got it!

It's elementary!

Alice has black and white feathers on her feather duster! That's it! That's the final piece of the jigsaw. It was Alice who burgled the ring. The feather proves it.

I must go and tell Sir Jeremy at once.

12pm

Dear Diary,

This day's gone from bad to worse. I presented Sir Jeremy with all of the evidence and explained logically how I know Alice was guilty. He was totally convinced. He called her in straight away and sacked her, effective today.

She was so very upset. So was Sir Jeremy. He loves all his staff. It must make him terribly sad to sack them.

Afterwards Alice cornered me in the kitchen. She pleaded with me: said she hadn't committed a crime, said we're making a terrible mistake, begged me to go back and talk to Sir Jeremy.

I didn't know what to say really. I like Alice - truly. But I can't change the facts.

As she was speaking, we heard Alfred cry out and then, shortly after, Sir Jeremy. They shouted for help; they said something terrible had happened. We hurried as fast as we could and found Ralph, who'd been guarding Sir Jeremy's office, passed out on the floor, a pool of dog sick next to him. Alice was very, very upset. She loved that dog.

Inside the office, Sir Jeremy's bureau was broken, the drawer was forced open and £100 missing. What a huge sum of money! Things were escalating quickly.

We called for a vet and for Constable Brighouse and both of them came very quickly. The vet said that Ralph had been poisoned. POISONED! He didn't know what with, probably something natural, and he gave him some fluids and he said he'd pull through. Alice was relieved. She hugged the vet who didn't return the gesture.

Constable Brighouse said the case was very serious. £100 was a lot of money. It happened in daylight, with nobody else present. This time it was certain, there was definitely a thief in our midst. He asked if we had any suspicions.

"Simple!" said Alfred. "We already know who the thief is: Alice. Charlotte unmasked her only this morning."

"Very well, Alice. You're coming with me!" Constable Brighouse put his handcuffs on Alice.

"Charlotte," she cried. "You don't think I'd hurt Ralph do you? Charlotte do something, I'm totally innocent."

I didn't have any time to reply before she was packed into the police van and driven off to prison.

Alfred went out on the driveway to wave. It almost seemed as if he was happy, but I'm probably mistaken.

I went back inside and found Sir Jeremy sat with his ransacked bureau in pieces quietly sobbing into a hanky. I told him not to worry, that we'd get back his money by hook or by crook.

He snapped at me. "Charlotte, you fool! I don't care about money. That's not what's important. I'm crying because someone poisoned our friend, Ralph. It could have been much worse; he could be a dead one. One healthy Ralph is worth all of my money. Oh Charlotte, I do hope he gets better soon."

9.30pm

Dear Diary,

What a day. I'm exhausted!
Ralph will pull through and the criminal is behind bars.
Two mysteries solved in one day… even Sherlock never did that!
It's all in a day's work for *Charlotte Holmes, Super Detective.*

Now, on top of **The Mystery of the Broken Biscuit Barrel** I can add **The Mystery of the Missing Ring** and **The Mystery of the Poisoned Dog.**

At this rate I'll have my own case book by Christmas.

Watch out Uncle Sherlock, I'm hot on your heels!

13 SECOND THOUGHTS

Thursday 15th September 1939

Dear Diary,

Johnson came to see me this morning. I don't think I've ever seen him inside the house before. He looked very sad and grey. He said he hadn't slept a wink all night. Poor man! He was in a terrible state.

We sat in the dining room and he poured out his heart. He pleaded with me, said he knew Alice was innocent. He said I was his only chance to get justice. He'd been to Sir Jeremy but had been turned away. He'd been to the jail but Constable Brighouse told him that unless the charges are dropped Alice has to stay locked up until there's a trial.

He begged me to speak to them. He told me they'd listen to me. He promised to give me more evidence, anything I needed. He told me he loved Alice more than anything else, he couldn't bear seeing her spend one more day in that prison for a crime she didn't commit.

He explained that the night Sir Jeremy's ring had gone missing Alice and he had been out on a date. They hadn't said earlier for fear Alfred would sack them, but the truth was he'd driven her up into the hills where they looked up at the stars and ate cheese and held hands. He told me she <u>couldn't</u> have stolen the ring.

He said that she had no motive to steal the ring. Yes, she liked jewelry, but she didn't have to steal it, because Johnson had saved up to buy her the ring of her dreams. He told me how he was planning to propose at the fête with a beautiful diamond ring. That's why he'd had that catalogue in the glove box.

As for the poisoned dog, he flat out denied she would ever do anything like that. It's true, she did love Ralph, and you'd have to be big and strong to break open the bureau. Alice did not look very big and strong.

The more he talked, the more doubts crept into my mind.

He produced from his pocket a letter... from Alice, asking how could I think she would do all these things? I could see where her teardrops had fallen on the page. I wondered – *how could I think she would do all of these things?* I had doubts in my heart.

So I wondered what Sherlock would do. He'd say there's no place for emotions. You must stick with the evidence.

Could Sherlock be wrong? Is that terrible advice?

As Johnson continued, my mind and heart raced away from each other in opposite directions. I listened and felt very confused.

In the end I just didn't know what to say. I just wished him luck and said I'd look into it.

He wasn't happy with that.

Neither was I.

I have no idea where to look next.

14 SYCAMORE

Friday 16th September 1939

5am

Dear Diary,

I have had the worst night's sleep. I kept waking up and thinking about Alice. Rethinking all of the evidence – have I missed anything out? I even tried to read my Sherlock Holmes book, but every sentence reminds me of Alice. Every page talks about evidence, crimes and confessions.

Dawn's only just breaking and I'm already wide awake, my head simply buzzing with thoughts. And more stones in my stomach. I have to do something. One way or another I have to find more evidence. I feel like I'm missing a piece of the jigsaw and I don't even know which one it is.

What's that? A tap-tap-tap at my window. It's probably Henry throwing stones. At dawn. If I ignore him he'll go away. It's far too early and I'm not in the mood.

Hang on – it's getting louder and louder. I'm going to have to go see what he wants.

7.30am

Dear Diary,

The knocking this morning – it turned out it wasn't Henry at all! It was Doug on his special long ladders. He said he wanted me to look at a sycamore tree. I told him we'd already looked at plenty of sycamore trees and I'd learned all the facts on the poster as well. He said I had so much more to learn, he told me to come and look.

He was very persistent. I gave my excuses:

1. It was 5 in the morning,
2. I was wearing pyjamas,
3. I had done enough tree climbing this week already.

Unfortunately, Doug wouldn't accept any excuses, and by sheer force of will I found myself in pyjamas and wellies carrying one end of a 40 foot ladder across a field at five o'clock in the morning. He set up the ladder and told me to get up and to pay careful attention to where the boughs meet the trunk.

As I climbed up, I remember thinking "Doug is a nice man, but Doug is also a strange man. Nothing about this makes any sense."

Then I saw. And then suddenly everything made perfect sense.

I gave an almighty cheer that bounced through the branches.

"You see it then?" Doug asked.

I cheered again.

"Aye, you seen it," he muttered to himself.

In the branches of the sycamore tree was a large empty nest. The birds had all left, but I knew which birds had been there. There had clearly been magpies, you could tell by the feathers they'd left behind: lovely black and white feathers. Just like the one that Sir Jeremy found in his room. And there, large as life in the bottom of the nest, was a wonderful shiny black and gold ring. Sir Jeremy's ring! There was no mistaking it.

Those cheeky, thieving magpies! They do love shiny things. One of them must have flown through the window and lifted the ring back to its nest.

This was it. There was no doubt any more. This was the missing piece of the puzzle.

I shouted out, "Doug, you're a genius!"

He replied: "I don't know 'bout that. I'm just being observant. When I spotted it this morning, I thought you'd want to know sharpish."

"You were right, Doug," I answered. "To the jail immediately! Call Johnson; we're going to need a lift."

Someone's beep-beeping. That must be Johnson now. I'll finish this later.

7pm

Dear Diary

What a difference a day makes.

I took the ring into the jail, and explained everything. Once

Constable Brighouse understood, he released Alice. She came running out into the street and Johnson gave her a hug and a great big kiss.

I told Alice how sorry I was, and how I felt ashamed that I ever thought she could have committed such a terrible crime. She could have been horrible to me, but she wasn't at all. She just smiled and said she understood and that we could still be friends.

By the time we got home, Sir Jeremy was up. He was surprised to see Alice out of jail and back at Batley Hall. We talked over breakfast, I explained about Doug and the magpies, the ring and all of the evidence. He was most intrigued.

When I'd got to the end, I produced from my pocket his ring and placed it back onto his finger. You should have seen his face light up. He was happy - so happy. He jumped up and started to sing an improvised song about having his ring back – dancing around the dining room as he did so.

He hugged Alice tight and begged her forgiveness.

And once again everyone was back on the same side.

Well, nearly everyone.

If Alice in innocent, then who did poison Ralph and burgle the bureau? Somewhere amongst us, there's a rotten apple. The final thing to do is to find them out.

I'll worry about that later. My next thing to do is to get some sleep.

15 THE FÊTE

Saturday 17th September 1939

8am

Dear Diary,

The day is finally here. The day of the Batley fête!

Everyone in the whole of Batley is going. We're all very excited. Henry and I have been looking at the programme in the parish news over breakfast.

There are so many fun things to do.

Obviously, there's Mrs Mirfield's cake stall. I can't wait to try some. They look super delicious. They're bound to raise loads of money for the church funds.

There are Morris dancers, Punch and Judy, and Farmer Thickett's dog and duck display.

There are plenty of stalls: tombola, hook a duck, ferret racing and an unlucky dip (on account of the rationing). Even Alfred's volunteered to do a splat-the-rat! It looks very professional: eight tubes and goodness known how many rats. It should be fun.

Doug is judging the vegetable contest. He's very excited. There's been a lot of anticipation for Mrs Scallion's spring onions. Last Sunday in church Rev Kindly said if they were any bigger they'd have to be called summer onions. It was quite the highlight of the service.

It's so exciting, and more importantly, I'm getting to spend it with all my friends… together again at last.

I'm looking forward to having a day off from sleuthing. It'll be nice to just have fun and relax.

8pm

Dear Diary,

For entertainment, I give Batley fête: 10

For relaxation: 2

It was all very pleasant until right near the end. When Rev Kindly announced the fundraising total he stood at the front of the church and lifted a huge tin of money and shook it so it jangled. You could tell there was an awful lot of money in it just by the face he pulled trying to lift it. Mrs Mirfield had sold loads of her cakes, and there'd been a lot spent on the other stalls too.

He did the usual kind of speech that vicars like to give. He thanked people for coming and for entering the contests. He invited Doug up to present the awards.

Doug was a natural – everyone loved him… slight hiccup when he awarded first place ornamental turnip to a woman who hadn't entered a turnip, but had a baby with an usually shaped head and had pushed her pram past at the critical moment.

You can imagine the uproar from the other entrants. We all had to wait while the senior officials rejudged all sixteen entries and picked a real turnip to win it. They awarded the baby third place which was nice, so they didn't go home empty handed.

Then the big moment, Rev Kindly lifted the tin and revealed a total collection of one hundred pounds. The audience gasped. It was an awful lot of money.

Then, just at that moment, an air raid siren sounded, and everybody quickly took cover.

Now the thing about having an air raid siren in a fête is that there aren't many good places to take cover. Fêtes have a lot of things made out of fabric which, as materials go, is not well known for providing protection from explosives.

I hid behind the tea and cake stall. It wasn't so safe, but I could see other people who had much less cover. Sir Jeremy hid behind the Punch and Judy booth. Ralph hid behind the unlucky dip. Thank goodness there weren't any planes (though it did seem a little strange.) All it would take was one bomb and there'd be nothing left but bunting and ferrets.

We must have been hiding for nine or ten minutes. When the all clear sounded, everyone came back to the green and Rev Kindly picked up where he stopped - EXCEPT someone had stolen the collection tin!

Imagine all that money vanished.

Rev Kindly was very upset. So was everyone. else They'd worked very hard to raise all of that money. It wasn't fair that someone should steal it.

Nobody knew who it was. How could we? We were all hiding.

No one had the foggiest what they should do. Then Sir Jeremy grabbed my arm and marched me up to the front.

He lifted my hand in the air and addressed the crowd. "People of Batley, do not despair! I'd like to recommend to you Charlotte Holmes. Not only is Charlotte the great niece of the famous super detective Sherlock Holmes. She is a super detective in her own right. Why, over these past two weeks she's solved three big mysteries already. If anyone can get to the bottom of this mess it's Charlotte."

There were a few scattered cheers and a round of applause. Then it was quiet.

Everybody was looking at me expectantly. It made me quite nervous. I cleared my throat and said in my loudest voice "Sir Jeremy flatters me. I'm sorry, he's wrong. I don't know how to solve this. It could have been anyone... anyone at all. Everyone in the Batley is here. I can rule out me, Sir Jeremy, Alice and two or three others I could see from where I was. But that would still leave us with hundreds of suspects."

I felt Sir Jeremy's hand on my back, and he leaned in and quietly whispered to me "All you need is a different point of view, Charlotte. I believe in you. Believe in yourself."

Those words stuck in my head. *"All you need is a different point of view."* Then it hit me.

IT WAS ELEMENTARY!

I addressed the crowd "Nobody move. Nobody speak. Vicar fetch me some paper and 600 pencils. Mrs Mirfield, empty the tombola barrel."

Rev Kindly strode off and was back in a jiffy with a giant box filled to the brim with stationery. We handed them out, then I asked everyone present to remember who they could see from their hiding place during the siren. Then each person was to write down those names on a slip of paper, come up and deposit their slip in the tombola barrel.

It didn't take long before everyone had answered.

Once more I addressed the congregation: "Let's think logically: what do we know? Everybody in the whole of Batley was here. Which means that whoever stole the money was also at the fête. And whoever it was, while they were stealing the money, the one thing they weren't doing was hiding. True, I could only see three or four people, but each of those people could see different people. As long as everybody was seen by at least one person, we'd be left with one person whom nobody saw and that must be the person who stole the money. Now please pay attention and if I read your name, sit on the floor till the barrel is empty."

I picked out a ticket and read out the names. One by one each of the people whose name was called sat down. Ticket by ticket we worked through the names. Some names were repeated, but that didn't matter as long as they stayed seated until the end.

The closer I got to the end of the barrel the fewer and fewer the people left standing… until only two people remained: Doug and Alfred. I drew the last ticket on which four names were written… and one of those names was Doug's.

"Doug, sit down!"

The crown started to murmur. Big strong Alfred looked ever so vulnerable stood all alone with the rest of the townsfolk sat down around him.

"Alfred," I continued "I put it to you that the only reason nobody could see you hiding is because you weren't really hiding. Instead, you were stealing the church money. PC Brighouse, arrest that man!"

PC Brighouse was there in a flash, waving his handcuffs in the air and reading Alfred his rights.

Alfred exploded: "Oh, is that it? Just because nobody saw me hiding, you think I stole the money? This doesn't prove anything! Maybe I just found a really good hiding place… or a bad hiding place surrounded by shortsighted people? How do you know I'm not just naturally camouflaged? I've might have won national awards in hide and seek!"

PC Brighouse chimed in: "He's right, Charlotte. If we don't find the money, we'll have to let him go free."

"Logically, what do we know?" I began "He's been here all along, so the money must be here as well. If I had to hide a hundred pounds in change, where would I hide it? Somewhere it wouldn't be found accidentally, stolen or mixed up with somebody else's property. It would have to be sealed up, and look unappealing, something that nobody else in their right minds would steal. Socks!"

Gasps and the word "socks!" rippled around the audience.

"It's perfect" I carried on "No-one would open old socks, no-one would steal them and no one would ever mistake them for theirs because ours are already on our feet."

 Then people started to titter. The titter grew into a laugh and the laugh grew into guffaws.

Someone I didn't recognise stood up in the middle. The crowd shushed themselves and the man began speaking.

"Did you see how much money was in that tin? You'd need a hundred socks to fit it all in. What on earth has a hundred socks? A chilly centipede?"

I answered "How about a very well stocked splat-the-rat? Officer, open those rats!"

PC Brighouse marched over to the splat-the-rat and ripped open the first rat he found. A cascade of change flew into the air.

Sir Jeremy bellowed "And that cracks the case of Charlotte Holmes and the Mystery of the Air Raid Siren. Officer – please take this man to prison!"

As the sirens of the police van faded in the distance, the crowd cheered. And just for that moment I felt like I was on top of the world.

Then, a single voice from the crowd pierced the moment of glory. "Wait!" It was Johnson. "There's still very important question we don't have an answer to…"

Unease spread through the crowd.

Johnson retrieved a box from his pocket, and out of the box took a large sparkly ring, every bit as unique and impressive as Sir Jeremy's signet ring. He turned to Alice, got down on one knee and said "Alice, I don't want to hide our love any more. I love you. And I want us to be together, forever. Will you do me the honour and marry me?"

"Yes!" Alice replied.

There was cheering and clapping and slaps on the back. The accordion player started playing a polka and the Morris men began an impromptu dance.

When all the festivities were well underway, Sir Jeremy and Rev Kindly carried on ripping up Alfred's splat-the-rat game. As well as the rest of the church money, inside the other socks they found Sir Jeremy's money from the bureau drawer and a bottle of home-made-oak-tree-dog-poison. So it WAS Alfred after all who poisoned poor Ralph and framed poor Alice.

What a horrible man. At least now we know he's going to be in prison for a very long time.

Once all the money was back in, Sir Jeremy stood up to make a speech.

'I'd like to thank all of you for being here today and making this

year's Batley fête the best one yet.

We've got the collection money back and with my hundred pounds that I'm adding to it, we've raised over £200 towards the church funds. That should be enough to keep Rev Kindly in cups of tea for a year.

But there is one person who most deserves our congratulations, ladies and gentlemen: young Charlotte Holmes. Step forward Charlotte.

Like your great-uncle Sherlock, you will go down in history as a super detective. Logical, observant and open minded. One day, all the children of Britain will read of your great cases:

The Mystery of the Broken Biscuit Barrel

The Mystery of the Missing Ring

The Mystery of the Poisoned Dog

The Mystery of the Air-Raid Siren

And many, many more to come, I'm sure.

Thank you, Charlotte, from the bottom of my heart. You've been very brave and very clever. And what's more important, you've learned to be confident. Now, it is my great pleasure to present to you this medal from all the people of Batley. Well done, Charlotte Holmes, SUPER DETECTIVE!"

And that's how I wound up getting a medal.

After that, everyone wanted to shake my hand and tell me how I was going to end up like my great Uncle Sherlock. I've never had to shake hands with 600 people before. It is rather exhausting.

I was pleased to get back to Batley Hall and write it all up in my diary.

Wowsers, diary, I am so tired! It'll be bedtime soon, so I'll have to stop here for now.

Besides, I've got something else much more important to write…

A letter for Mum: to let her know I haven't forgotten her face.

ABOUT THE AUTHOR

Ben Richards is a playwright and theatre maker from Salford. He spent ten years as a school teacher before launching a new career writing for young people and family audiences.

He is a previous winner of the PMA Writer's Award.

Together with Will Cousins he runs The Big Tiny Productions creating magical theatrical experiences for the whole family to enjoy.

Printed in Poland
by Amazon Fulfillment
Poland Sp. z o.o., Wrocław

65071294R00061